Adina
at Her
Best

Menucha Publishers, Inc.
© 2019 by Rebecca Klempner
Typeset and designed by Adam Komosinski
All rights reserved

ISBN 978-1-61465-518-3
Library of Congress Control Number: 2018960849

Published and distributed by:
Menucha Publishers, Inc.
1235 38th Street
Brooklyn, NY 11218
Tel/Fax: 718-232-0856
www.menuchapublishers.com
sales@menuchapublishers.com

Printed in the United States

Adina at Her Best

Rebecca Klempner

To every kid (and adult) who has ever gotten distracted,
had trouble looking without touching,
struggled to listen without spacing out,
or spoken without thinking first.

Contents

CHAPTER 1

A Note of Apology

I'm halfway out the door of our classroom on Tuesday afternoon when Mrs. Sabban calls out, "Adina, can you stay here for a moment?"

My best friend, Henny, whispers, "I'll meet you by the water fountain, okay?" I nod.

Turning around, I look Mrs. Sabban in the eye. "Yes?"

"I heard you were really rude to Mrs. Rubin when she subbed yesterday." She takes off her glasses, pinches the bridge of her nose, and sighs. During this pause, I hear the cheerful clamor of girls in the hallway, heading home, sharing jokes, making plans. I wish I were out there, anywhere, not here.

As Mrs. Sabban puts the glasses back on, she continues. "Mrs. Rubin said you told her that you didn't have to listen to her because she's not a real teacher."

I'd forgotten about that. Honestly, I forget a lot of the things I say as soon as I say them. If only the people I say them to could forget them as easily. "She yelled at me because I wasn't working. But I was working. I just hadn't finished yet."

"Yes, I noticed you didn't complete the workbook pages she assigned."

"I could hear the girls in 3-A rehearsing their performance next door." In a week, they'll be putting on the annual grade three production. "I was distracted." I was more than distracted: I sang along with all the words, under my breath, remembering myself standing on the stage singing last year.

Mrs. Sabban sinks down in the chair at her desk. I notice the circles under her eyes and the way her lipstick has smeared just a bit. She takes out a folder. Flipping it open, she removes a sheet of paper — nice, heavy paper, cream colored. "I can't let you treat a sub with such disrespect, Adina. It sends a wrong message — to you, and to the other students." Now she opens a drawer, takes out a red felt-tip. She writes a small x at the bottom of the page, then draws a line next to it.

Handing the sheet of paper to me, she says, "You will write Mrs. Rubin an apology on this piece of stationery tonight. I want you to write at least five sentences. And

I want you to follow the 'friendly letter' format — it's in your English book. When you're done, one of your parents should sign on the line I just drew at the bottom."

I notice there's a sticky note attached to the paper with Mrs. Rubin's full name and address. Who knew her name is Fradl?

Mrs. Sabban clears her throat, and I look back at her. "If you don't bring me the letter tomorrow morning, you can't go on the field trip on Thursday."

"What?!" I say one nasty thing to a teacher — a sub! — and Mrs. Sabban won't let me go to Rancho Los Cerritos? We've been studying California history for weeks and weeks. This is supposed to be the payoff!

"You're going to finish the letter, Adina. And your parents will sign it. And then you will hand it in tomorrow morning. I'll put a stamp on it, and together we'll drop it in the mailbox at the corner." Mrs. Sabban's voice is firm. "Don't start panicking about the field trip."

My hands shaking, I sling my backpack onto a desk. I unzip it and prepare to slide the paper between two plastic binders.

"Put it inside a folder, Adina. It needs to stay neat and flat. And remember your English book."

Slipping my backpack back on, I shuffle toward the door.

Behind me, I hear Mrs. Sabban's chair slide across the floor as she stands up. "You're going to write a beautiful letter, Adina. And on Thursday you'll be on the bus with the rest of us, you'll see."

I don't look at her on the way out.

"WHAT HAPPENED IN THERE?" Henny says when I finally catch up with her. "I've been waiting forever!"

"Mrs. Sabban gave me some fancy paper."

Henny makes a *bracha* — a blessing — then bends forward and slurps some water from the fountain. The machine rumbles. "Why would she do that?"

"I have to write an apology to Mrs. Rubin."

"For what?"

"Talking back. When she yelled at me for spacing out."

"Everyone knows you're a daydreamer." Henny throws her hands in the air. "I don't know why she decided to make a big deal of it."

As my face heats up, we start toward the exit. *Everyone knows I'm a daydreamer?* It's not like it isn't true; it is. It's just the idea that the other girls have noticed. I wish Henny hadn't said anything.

"We're late getting Nachum," I say, rather than, *Hey! I thought you were on my side!*

Outside, it's a typically sunny afternoon in Los Angeles; there's hardly a cloud in the sky, and the weather is pleasantly warm, but not hot. We weave in and out of all the kids and parents loitering around the Girls' Building of Torah MiKedem Academy. When Henny and I reach the corner of Detroit and Clinton, she says, "Is that all? You just write an apology? Can she even make you do that?"

"If I don't, I can't go on the field trip."

Henny gasps. "But we were going to sit together! And share nosh!" Little furrows pop up in her forehead. "I bought a bag of those sweet popcorn thingies you like!"

I shrug. "Don't worry…I'll just write the apology."

The clouds on Henny's face clear. "Good." She squeezes me, real quick, and all my annoyance with her disappears.

While we walk to the Boys' Building to pick up my younger brother, Henny tells me about a book she's been reading. She says, "It's the best!" and "You've got to read it!" and mentions all sorts of characters I know nothing about. I make little nods and *uh-huh*s so she thinks I'm listening. But in the back of my head, I worry. What's going to happen if I forget to write the letter? I imagine everyone else leaving on the big yellow school bus Mrs. Sabban and Mrs. Friend hired to drive all the fourth graders to Rancho Los Cerritos — while I stand under the palm tree next to the school. All the girls watch me through the windows of the bus, waving at me as the bus drives away…

I've got to write that letter! But writing is so hard,

and takes so long, and it's the last thing I want to do on a sunny spring afternoon in Los Angeles. I don't even remember to do my homework most of the time. Or I start it, but I don't finish.

I'll just write it first, I think. *Even if I don't finish my homework, I'll finish the letter.*

"Adina!" Henny calls out. "Green light!"

Startled, I start across the street, a few steps behind her. But not far enough to miss her saying, "Spaced out again, eh?"

When we get home, I drop my backpack on the floor in the foyer and kick off my shoes: one, two. Then, I stop briefly in front of the mirror to adjust my favorite, perfect headband, and head to the kitchen. I need food before my brain can deal with homework.

Barely looking at my big sister, Michal, who has parked herself at the table with a stack of books, I rummage through the fridge for the perfect snack. There's a piece of leftover pizza, but I'm not in the mood. But maybe…

"Michal? Can you make me a smoothie?" I ask without turning around.

"Too busy," she says.

Yogurt, then. Yogurt is healthy and yummy and much more convenient. I grab a container and a dairy spoon, lean against the counter, mumble a quick *bracha*, and dig in.

Michal looks up for a minute. "Mom says she'll be home at five thirty or so." My mother's a dentist, and she usually spends a couple afternoons at her office to see patients whose parents don't want them to miss school for a dental appointment.

Nachum comes in and flings open the refrigerator door. "Pizza! Score!" While he does a little dance of celebration, the phone rings. I pick it up.

"Aunt Nitzan!" I say, after she identifies herself. "How are you? And the baby?"

"*Baruch Hashem* — Thank God — I'm fine. And the baby — just amazing!" Aunt Nitzan spends the next fifteen minutes telling me all the ways in which the baby is just amazing. And when I hang up the phone, I remember that last night I stopped reading my library book right before Bina Gold revealed the guilty party. I want to know who it was, so I head to my bedroom and curl up with the book.

CHAPTER 2

Whoops!

After lunch on Wednesday, Mrs. Sabban crosses the yard to pick us up from recess as usual. When she reaches us, she looks at me and raises an eyebrow. Is she expecting something from me? When I don't respond, she looks disappointed. Turning on her heel, she leads us into the building.

Henny nudges me with a pointy elbow. "You brought the letter?"

The letter!

I meant to write it last night; really, I did! But when I finished my mystery yesterday, Nachum showed me the prize — a fun card game — he'd earned from his rebbi, and we'd played until dinner. And then, after dinner, he did his homework. And Michal did her homework. And

Yosef did his homework. And I read another overdue library book.

"Adina," Mrs. Sabban says, as she goes up and down the rows of desks in our classroom, stamping the folders of all the girls who have brought in their homework. "Homework today?"

I shake my head, firmly, twice. I keep my eyes on my desk. They are filling with tears.

"The letter?" Mrs. Sabban sounds surprised. I guess she thought her threat was so serious that I would make sure to write the letter. And I meant to, I did…

"Do you still have the stationery?" Mrs. Sabban whispers. At this point, some of the girls have noticed our conversation. I feel them watching me and wish I could disappear.

My face hotter than July, I whisper back, "It's still in my folder."

"Good." Mrs. Sabban walks to the next desk, stamps Zeesie Marks's folder. "Don't forget."

Henny comes over to me, holding out a tissue. I wipe my tears.

The next ten minutes are a blur. I'm not really paying attention to the novel Mrs. Sabban is reading to us, but she seems to know I need to be left alone. I just sit there, looking around at the bulletin boards and classroom decorations, half-listening.

When Mrs. Sabban asks us to get out our spelling

books, I feel a little better. I even manage to finish all my seatwork today.

On the way out of class, Mrs. Sabban stops me. "Would you like to stay, Adina? To write the letter?" Her eyebrows snap together over concerned eyes. "I'm going to be here, grading papers, for about a half an hour. If you write the letter here, you won't be able to forget."

I look up at Mrs. Sabban. Usually, I think of her as strict. For the first time, I realize that maybe she is kind too. She doesn't want me to fail. She just wants me to learn my lesson. And for a second, I am going to accept her offer.

But then I remember: I have to pick up Nachum. He's waiting for me. Yesterday, when Henny and I were late to his classroom, he was steamed.

Reluctantly, I shake my head. "My brother is waiting for me."

Henny approaches from the cubbies and stands next to me. "I won't let her forget."

Today, we pick up Nachum on time. As we walk home, I hum to myself. I'm sure Henny and Nachum think I'm singing one of the Pirkei Avot songs from the third grade play again. And I am, sort of, but this time I've changed the words:

The letter, the letter, don't forget the letter. The letter, the letter, you've got to write the letter...

CHAPTER 3

A Chat with Mom and Dad

When Nachum and I get home, Mom's still at her office. But Michal's already in the kitchen, doing her homework at the table. The sight of Michal doing her homework reminds me of mine. I know it's hard to believe, but I almost forgot again.

Without stopping at the fridge for a snack, without picking up a book or a toy, I pull the folder from my backpack, take out the sheet of fancy paper — stationery, Mrs. Sabban called it — and look around for a pen.

"What's that?" Nachum's hand is already deep in a bag of potato chips.

"None of your business," I snap. *Aha!* There's a pen in the mug with the broken handle sitting on the counter by the phone. I snatch it up and turn back to the table. Crumbs dot its surface, and a smudge of peanut butter or hummus or something. I get a damp paper towel and wipe them away. Then I spread out my paper, sit in the creaky old chair, and think back to Monday.

The truth is, Mrs. Rubin was boring. She didn't tell us wacky stories like other subs, or have neat experiments or art projects like Mrs. Sabban. There were just worksheets and reading — silent reading — and nothing to get us moving around or laughing. Mrs. Rubin was boring, boring, boring, and I couldn't pay attention. It just wasn't possible.

And then she screamed at me. As if I was trying to be *chutzpahdik* — rude. But I wasn't. I was just spacing out.

I wasn't getting my work done, but I wasn't disturbing anyone, was I? Okay, maybe Leah Gurwitz, but she knows she can just kick my chair to tell me I'm annoying her, and I'll apologize, and then we'll be all fair and square.

When someone screams at me, I just want to scream right back. I know it's not right, but the words just jumped out of my mouth. And once they were out, I couldn't stuff them back in.

"Are you all right?" Michal says. "You have a funny look on your face."

"I'm just thinking." But I'm not. I've pictured the scene

with Mrs. Rubin so clearly, I feel the rush of anger her screaming let loose in me. My heart is racing, and I just want to yell at someone, anyone.

"Hmm." Michal looks at me for a moment, considering me with one eyebrow raised. Then she turns back to whatever math problem she's been working on. She's so advanced in math, the problem looks like a magic spell, full of squiggly lines and mysterious symbols. My parents aren't sure what the school will do once Michal completes all the math courses they normally offer. Oh, the troubles of the brilliant and well behaved!

By now, Nachum has his Torah volume out. He starts to chant the verses he learned in school today.

How can I think in this ruckus?

"Can you keep it down?" I ask.

Nachum just keeps singing.

"Nachum!"

He looks up.

"I need to think."

"Can you do your thinking somewhere else? I'm doing my homework." And then he starts all over again.

So I hit him.

"Hey!" Nachum hits me back. He's only eight, but his slap hurts.

Looking up from her homework, Michal says, "Cut it out or I'll tell Mom. And then you'll both be punished."

I fling my pen down and it leaves a spot of ink on the stationery.

I burst into tears.

Michal sighs and puts down her pencil. "Adina, can you at least explain what's bothering you? We can't help you if you don't explain."

When I wipe my face on my sleeve, she wrinkles her nose in disgust, but I get the feeling she really wants to help me.

"I got in trouble for being mean to the sub we had for English on Monday. Yesterday, Mrs. Sabban asked me to write a note to the sub, you know, to apologize. But I forgot. So now I have to write an apology letter *tonight*, or I can't go on our field trip tomorrow."

"The fourth-grade field trip? The one to Rancho Los Cerritos?"

"That's the one."

"I wouldn't want to miss it either." She taps her chin with the eraser end of her sparkly pink pencil.

"Mrs. Sabban says I have to write the letter in real 'friendly letter' format."

"Did you learn that yet?"

"Yeah. And I brought my book home to help." I fish around in my backpack and locate the book. It takes a minute or two, but we eventually find the page we need.

Michal tears a piece of lined paper out of her notebook.

"It would be smart to write a rough draft. You want to get the wording right before you go writing in pen on that piece of stationery."

I moan. Two drafts? Why does writing anything take so long?

But Michal walks me though the whole thing. She helps me think of the exact words to use, shows me how to write neatly on the unlined sheet of paper. Even Nachum gets involved — he corrects my spelling when I spell "awful" and "disrespectful" wrong.

By the time Mom gets home, I've written five complete sentences and signed my apology in cursive. I still have the rest of my homework to do, but at least I'm done writing the letter. I'm about to slip it into my folder when I realize I have to ask Mom to sign it.

And then she's going to know I got in trouble in school again.

My heart falls faster than a baby bird tumbling from a nest when it's not quite ready to fly. *Splat.*

Every time a teacher complains about my incomplete assignments, my calling out in class, my disorganized desk, it's one more reason for Mom to be disappointed in me. She never yells (well, hardly ever) but I can tell from her groans, her lips pressed together, that she doesn't approve of how I act at school. She's not so fond of how I act at home sometimes either.

I wait until Mom has slipped a foil pan of lasagna into the oven to show her the letter. As she reads it, I can see her pupils move back and forth, following each line across the page.

Closing her eyes, Mom takes a deep breath. "Fradl Rubin? You were rude to Fradl Rubin?" She opens her eyes.

I wince. Then, slowly, I nod.

Mom sighs again, then goes to the broken mug for a pen. She signs the letter on the red line below my name and thrusts it toward me like it smells bad or something. Silently, I put it in my folder.

"I've got something for you to sign too!" Nachum says. He pulls out his three-ring binder, pops it open, and removes a sheet of paper.

Mom beams the moment she spots the grade at the top. "You got 102? That's great!"

"I got both the extra credit questions too."

She musses his hair. "That's my kid!"

Jealousy grabs hold of me. Why did he have to show Mom that test now? Couldn't he have waited until after dinner?

I kick him under the table.

His grin vanishes.

Before Mom can notice, I ask her, "Do you want me to set the table?"

Turning toward me, she says, "Sure, Adina. That would be very helpful."

I rush to the cabinet to grab the dairy plates. Just then, the phone rings. Michal answers it. After a second, she holds it out toward me. "For you. It's Henny."

I take the phone from my sister. "Thanks."

"Did you write the letter?" Henny asks, sounding anxious.

"What do you think?"

"Oh, Adina! You can't put if off any longer, Mrs. Sabban isn't going to—"

Great. Even my best friend doesn't believe in me. "Relax, Hen. I just put it in my folder a few minutes ago."

"*Baruch Hashem!*"

"See you tomorrow, Henny."

"I sure will!"

LATER, AFTER DINNER, Mom and Dad ask me to meet them in the den for a "chat." A chat is supposed to be a casual, friendly conversation, but I suspect this chat is going to be serious, like the talk I had yesterday with Mrs. Sabban. I wish I could say, *No, thanks, I've got something else I'd rather do — like trim my toenails.* But I know that's not an option.

"Adina," Dad starts as he plops onto the overstuffed green plaid chair we think of as "Dad's chair" and puts his feet up on a matching ottoman, "your mother and I are worried about you. We've noticed you are struggling at school. At home too."

"What do you mean?"

Mom sits on the arm of the chair. "Your room: it's so messy that you can't find things you need, like uniform shirts and pens and the books you've checked out from the school library. Do you know that yesterday I tripped over your backpack and shoes when I walked in from work? And it wasn't the first time."

I squirm. Unfortunately, her accusation sounds a little truer than I'd like.

"And when you are angry…do you know how often you hit Nachum? Or shove him? It's not appropriate at your age. You should know better." Mom gazes over my head at a photo of the Western Wall in Jerusalem on a snowy day. "And you say things, hurtful things, to all of us."

I can't look her in the eye. I feel small, smaller than a worm. "The words just fly out of my mouth—"

Dad taps me on the arm, very gently. "Sweetie, you are a good girl, a smart one and a kindhearted one. But when you're so impulsive, so disorganized, it makes it hard for people to appreciate your good qualities."

I take his words in. "So what can I do about it? I'm telling you, I try…I've *been* trying. But it's just the way I am."

Mom looks at me. She doesn't seem angry or disappointed anymore, just worried. "Honey, we want to take you to a special doctor, to do some testing."

"A doctor?"

Dad nods. "And a therapist too. They might be able to see what's going on. Maybe give you some tools to help you out."

My eyes fill with tears. "You don't love me the way I am."

"We don't want you to be anyone but you," Mom insists.

"But the real me has good bits and bad bits!"

Mom opens her mouth to reply, but Dad looks at her, and she closes it. He says, "We don't think there are any bad bits of you. We just think you need some," he pauses, looking for the right word, "*help* so you can keep all your *middot* — your character traits — in balance."

"I don't need help from some doctor."

Mom takes a big gulp. "We're willing to wait to make the appointment until you feel ready."

"I'm not ready!" My whole body is trembling with angry feelings. *My parents think I'm broken!*

Mom and Dad exchange a look. Then Dad says, "Let us know when you are."

I want to shout, *I'll never be ready!* But I satisfy myself by racing down the hallway and slamming my door.

CHAPTER 4

The Long Ride to Long Beach

It's Thursday morning, and I'm running late.

    I run late a lot, and usually it's not such a big deal. But I've got to get that letter to Mrs. Sabban as soon as possible!

I get my lunch box halfway packed and then realize I'm supposed to use a brown paper bag because of the trip. Running back to the freezer, I exchange my reusable ice pack for a frozen juice box. Then I grab a bag of pretzels. My hands are shaking so much that I dump some of them when I try to pour them into a plastic baggie.

Dad watches me over the row of cereal boxes in the center of the kitchen table. "Don't worry," he says. "I'll drop you off on my way to the office."

I finish packing my lunch with no more spills, then

stick it in my backpack. But where's my favorite head-band?! I run to the bathroom and frantically pull out one drawer after another to search for it.

"Looking for this?" Michal stands in the doorway, holding out my headband, which has a big blue bow that matches my uniform. "I found it under the couch."

"Thanks!" I say, snatching it from her hand and ignor-ing the implied accusation of sloppiness as I slip it over my bobbed hair.

Nachum and I follow Dad out of the house. We climb into the backseat of Dad's Volvo, but there's a colorful flyer on my seat.

"What's this?" I ask, pointing.

Dad looks over his shoulder. "Infographic. I made it to help our patients identify the symptoms of a stroke. You can just move it over." Dad works at a hospital.

I pick it up and settle into the seat. Nachum looks at the flyer, now in my lap. Across the top, it says in big magenta letters: *Act FAST to Respond to Stroke.* Below, it spells out the letters in *FAST.*

F — Ask them to smile. Is their face *unbalanced?*

A — Can they lift their arms *to the same height?*

S — Can they speak *clearly?*

T — Can they stick out their tongue *straight?*

Nachum asks, "So you do this little test, and then you can tell if someone's having a stroke?"

"Exactly," Dad replies, reversing the car out of the driveway cautiously.

"What's a stroke?" I ask.

Dad says, "When blood can't flow to the brain because of a blockage or if a blood vessel bursts. The cells in your brain can't survive without the oxygen in your blood."

"And then you die," Nachum adds. I'm not surprised he knows about strokes; he knows just about everything. Another Ben Ami genius.

"Sometimes," Dad says, and then he hesitates. I look at him in the rearview mirror. His mouth twists a bit. Then he adds, "It's what my father died of." His father died just a few days before Nachum was born. That's how my brother got his name: Nachum Eliyahu. Eliyahu was my grandfather's name. "By the time his buddies at shul realized what was happening, it was too late." Another pause, then, "It didn't matter that his son was a neurologist."

"So if the people around someone having a stroke figure out what's happening fast, it's less likely they'll die?"

"Yup." Dad parks the car at the curb near school. "You get the patient medicine quickly, you might save their life. You might even prevent them from having any lasting damage. But there are no guarantees."

I look at the clock. Yikes! Grabbing my backpack, I

say, "Thanks for the ride, Dad."

"Yeah," Nachum pipes up. "Thanks!"

Mrs. Sabban looks relieved when I hand her the letter for Mrs. Rubin. "Good job, Adina. We can mail it later."

When I sit down, Henny catches my eye and then pats her giant sweatshirt pocket. That must be where she packed the popcorn chips. Oh no! I forgot to grab extra nosh for the ride!

There's nothing I can do about it now. We are ready to get on the bus. I'm hoping to get seats near the back so we can sneak our chips on the way to the rancho. Several moms have joined us for the day. I hope they are laid-back and not bossy or strict.

"Okay, ladies!" Mrs. Friend, the other fourth-grade teacher, claps her hands. We all clap our hands back, then listen. "I want everyone to line up in two lines, side by side. Let's get on this bus quickly, and in an orderly fashion, so we can get on our way."

Henny and I stand next to each other near the front of the lines. She smiles at me, and I know from the way she is bouncing on her toes and the twinkle in her eye that she is excited — very excited.

"Adina!" Mrs. Sabban approaches, wearing hot pink sneakers rather than her usual ballet flats. "I want you sitting near the front, next to me."

I know what she's thinking: she wants to keep an eye on me. "I was hoping to sit with Henny."

"You can still sit with Henny, but across the aisle from me."

I blow out a puff of air. There goes our plan for the nosh.

"Take the first bench on the right side of the bus."

Henny looks at me and rolls her eyes. It's our turn to go up the steps. I let Henny go first and follow right away. No one's in the driver's seat. Curious, I look over my shoulder. Outside, Mrs. Friend is talking to a woman in a navy-blue uniform. Is that the driver?

"Move it, Ben Ami!" Shoshi Seligman, from the other fourth-grade class, is on my heels.

Grunting at her, I climb the last step and find Henny. She's sitting in the wrong seat — the first bench to the left, not the right. I raise an eyebrow at her.

"If we sit right behind the driver, we can't see anything. It'll be much more interesting if we can look out the front window."

She has a point. Besides, if you face the front of the bus, it is the right side. I drop onto the bench beside her. Hopefully, Mrs. Sabban won't mind.

The bus seat is made of bumpy dark-green vinyl. Leaning back against it, I start to sing under my breath.

"Quiet," Leora Cantor says as she makes her way

toward a seat.

I sing louder.

Henny whispers, "Don't get in trouble today, Adina! Mrs. Sabban might put you in another seat. Or make you sit with her!"

I cut my song short.

Eventually, all the girls, and the five mothers helping us out, have boarded the bus. Mrs. Sabban and Mrs. Friend get on. Mrs. Sabban sits at the front with the cooler containing the classes' brown bag lunches. She doesn't even seem to notice the little switcheroo that Henny made. Mrs. Friend starts toward the back of the bus, stopping halfway down the aisle. I guess we wouldn't have been able to hide back there, anyway.

She does her little clapping thing again, and then she says, "Now, ladies, we're going to be off-campus today. When a Jew is outside our community, it's important to make a good impression on the people around us. That means I want everyone on their very best behavior."

Oh no. It's hard enough pleasing my parents, my teachers — why do I have to worry about what some stranger thinks of me?

"We want all the people we see today to think Jewish girls are good girls and that our school is a school with well-behaved students."

I shoot Henny a look, but I don't get the response I'm

hoping for. She's watching Mrs. Friend and nodding.

I sigh.

Why can't a field trip just be fun?

Mrs. Friend makes it to the last row of the bus and sits down. Excited chatter fills the air.

There's a clatter at the door as the woman in the uniform who I saw earlier climbs the stairs. She's Black, and she's wearing a blue uniform.

"Good morning!" I say.

Her grin makes her very pretty, in an older, motherly way. "And good morning to you, sugar!"

Picking up a glittery pair of sunglasses from the dashboard, she settles into her big padded seat and slides the glasses over her ears. One finger with purple nail polish reaches up and pushes them up the bridge of her nose. She's wearing big hoop earrings too.

There's a clipboard attached to the side of her seat. Our driver checks something written on it — maybe the address of Rancho Los Cerritos? — and starts the motor.

Mrs. Sabban leans forward. "Shirley, how long do you think it'll take to get there?"

"I just checked the traffic. It'll be about an hour."

"Perfect! We'll be right on time!" Mrs. Sabban turns toward Henny and me. She must be pleased with what she sees, because she smiles, crosses her ankles, leans her head against her seat back, and closes her eyes.

Hmmm…a whole hour. What should we do?

While Shirley rolls us away from school, I turn and peer around the side of my seat. Some girls are playing Cat's Cradle; a little babyish, if you know what I mean. A couple have books. Some are playing finger games or hand claps. Elisheva Pinkus is French-braiding Sigal Shirazi's hair. Shoshi Seligman is telling a story and a bunch of girls are listening. The story must be funny; all the girls are laughing. Mrs. Friend appears to be praying, but just as I think she's not watching us, she peeks over the top of the book.

Now that we're on the road, there's lots to look at. I'm glad Henny picked out these seats. We can see the cars, the billboards, the shops lining La Brea Avenue.

"Is that a Ferrari?" I ask, pointing at a bright-yellow car in the next lane.

Henny shrugs.

"Sure is!" Shirley calls out from the driver's seat. "You like sports cars?"

"My oldest brother, Yosef, does. He taught me the names of his favorites." I look around at the traffic and point at another car. "That one's a Corvette."

Henny says, "Maybe we should count cars. You count all the red ones, and I count all the blue. Whoever has the highest number when we get to the rancho wins!"

I can't think of anything better to do, so I agree. We

spend the next hour counting cars. Occasionally, we can't decide if a car is dark blue or black, so we let Shirley decide. Mrs. Sabban opens an eye every few minutes. When she sees that we are on good behavior — our VERY BEST behavior — she shuts it again.

After forty-seven minutes — or so Miriam Schneider informed us all after she checked her new watch — we roll down a long, straight road that ends with a big sign announcing, "Rancho Los Cerritos." There are two roads forking off this dead end, one to the left and one to the right. Shirley turns left and pulls our bus into a parking lot.

In the parking lot, I get to add one more red car to my count of sixteen, but Henny has spotted a whopping sixty-five blue cars. "You won," I admit.

"What's my prize?" She bats her eyes at me.

"A deluxe trip to Rancho Los Cerritos!" I announce with exaggerated glee.

Laughing, Henny replies, "Just what I always wanted!"

Kneeling on my seat, I peek out the windows. I am not impressed by the view. Mostly, it's an ugly, dusty parking lot, with trees and bushes here and there. A train whistles, and I can hear it *chug-chug-chugging* nearby.

"Where's the house?" one of the girls calls out. After all, that's why we drove to Rancho Los Cerritos. There's an adobe house — we learned the word for the mud bricks used by settlers in Old California — and we're going to learn all about its history. But as I press my face against the window, I don't see a house.

Shirley turns off the motor, then sees me looking all around. "It's more interesting when you get inside. I promise." And she flashes another one of those pretty smiles.

"Are you coming with us?" Henny asks.

Standing up, Shirley stretches her legs. "Nah, but I've been driving fourth graders here for probably twenty years now. It's a real neat place. You'll take a tour, eat your lunch, and then I'll take you back to school. There's a nice place for me to sit, with picnic benches and all, and I've brought myself a book to read." She pats a pouch on the wall where she's stashed a paperback and a lunch box.

Mrs. Sabban stretches her arms over her head and stands up. "Ladies, please remain seated while I tell the guides that we're here."

Cranking open the door, Shirley lets her off the bus. We watch Mrs. Sabban walk out of the parking lot and toward the other road that led away from the dead end. It must lead to the rancho, I realize.

Meanwhile, I'm getting antsy. How long do we have to wait? I know I'm supposed to remain seated, but my legs feel scrunched up. So I stand.

"Adina Ben Ami!" Mrs. Friend calls out. "Sit back down, please."

As I flop back into my seat, I hear snickering. Are they

laughing at me?

"It won't be too much longer, dearie," Shirley tells me.

I slouch against my seat.

"Your name's Adina?" she asks. I nod. "That's a real pretty name. A Jewish name? I mean, it's Hebrew?"

"Yup. It means 'tender' or 'gentle.'" I know because we wrote a report on our names last year.

"That's very pretty. Very pretty, indeed. I have no idea what Shirley means, other than me." She winks, and I laugh.

Henny says, "My name is Henya. Only everyone calls me Henny."

"That so?" Shirley says.

"Uh-huh. And it's Yiddish, not Hebrew."

We hear something at the door and turn to look. It's Mrs. Sabban. And next to her is a man with a name tag. I hope this means our tour is finally going to begin.

CHAPTER 5

The Ranch of the Little Hills

The man with Mrs. Sabban is tall and skinny, and he has wrinkles around his eyes and mouth like he laughs a lot. His scruffy white hair is thinner on top and sticks out in every direction. A white mustache stands out against his tan face. He's got a name tag on his khaki shirt that reads "Martin Gonzales."

Mrs. Sabban climbs the steps at the front of the bus and claps her hands. We clap back. "Okay, everyone! I'd like to introduce you to Mr. Gonzales. He's our guide today. We're going to make two lines and walk to the front of the Visitor Center, where he'll tell us about the rancho. After that, we'll break up into smaller groups, and tour guides will lead us around the buildings and gardens. Let's exit the bus one row at a time, please."

That means Henny and I get off first. We struggle to our feet — my leg has fallen asleep, so I stomp my foot to wake it up before stumbling down the steps. As we're getting off the bus, Mr. Gonzales watches us with an unwavering smile.

"Did cowboys live here?" I ask. Henny elbows me, but not hard.

"They sure did," he says. "You'll hear all about it in a short while."

After everyone is off the bus, we march past the "Rancho Los Cerritos" sign. We left school at about nine, and now it's closer to ten and warming up. I start to sweat under my uniform, so when we reach the clearing in front of the small Visitor Center, I'm glad someone's put up a blue canopy to keep the sunshine off us.

"It looks like we've got everyone here now," Mr. Gonzales says. "Welcome to Rancho Los Cerritos! Right behind me is the Visitor Center. Let me tell you a little about the history of Rancho Los Cerritos before you enter the rancho and get a good look at it yourselves.

"Where you are standing today used to be the home of the Tongva people. They lived off the plentiful deer, fish, acorns, berries, and other foods native to this area. But after White people arrived, the Tongva fell ill from White people's diseases and were rounded up and forced to live on missions. They were forced to become Christian."

"Reminds me of the Spanish Inquisition," one of the mothers, Mrs. Azizi, whispers. The woman beside her, Mrs. Pelcowitz, nods her head.

"In 1784, the government gave a Spanish soldier, Manuel Nieto, a land grant of three hundred thousand acres as a reward for his military service. Nieto's family held the land until 1834. At that point, the land was divided into six so each of the Nieto children would get property of their own."

It's hard to focus on all the names and dates, and my mind starts to wander. I shake my head and try to focus on what Mr. Gonzales is saying.

"Nieto's daughter, Manuela Cota, received the area known as Rancho Los Cerritos. It means 'Ranch of the Little Hills.'"

"Ranch of the Little Hills?" I whisper to Henny. "Give me a break!"

She snickers.

"Why don't they call it something awesome, like 'Castle Magnificent'?"

She giggles some more, then offers, "Or how about 'Chateau de la Ooh-La-La'?"

I snort, and Mrs. Friend must hear us, because she turns around and wags a finger at us. I try to look as innocent as possible and pay more attention to Mr. Gonzales.

"Manuela Cota and her husband, Guillermo, built at least two adobes here. They had twelve children." *That reminds me of my great-grandmother, Malka — she had thirteen kids!* "But when Manuela died in 1843, her descendants decided they didn't want to live here. Instead, they sold Rancho Los Cerritos to a man named John Temple. Temple wanted the land to raise cattle for leather and tallow."

"Did cowboys live here?" I call out. Everyone looks at me, some with rolling eyes, but Mr. Gonzales grins extra wide, right at me.

"Yes, sirree! Only they weren't called cowboys. Does anyone know what the Mexicans called cowboys?"

Hands shoot up all around me. Mr. Gonzales points at Leora. "Vaqueros!" she says, triumphantly.

"Exactly right! And you'll learn all about the vaqueros during your tour." He waits for a second, then continues, "In 1866, there was a horrible drought. Can I have four students step to the front?" Four girls step forward. "Imagine each of these young ladies represents a quarter of Temple's herd. How many of them do you think survived that flood?"

Girls shout out guesses. I yell, "Three!"

"Well," Mr. Gonzales says to the girls, "if I point to you, pretend you're dead." He points to one, and she sticks out her tongue and slouches. We all laugh, but then he does it to a second girl, and then a third. We gasp. "Yup! Three-quarters of Temple's cattle died. He decided he'd had enough of the cattle business, and sold out to Flint, Bixby & Co. in 1866."

Honestly, I can't keep all those names and numbers straight, but Mr. Gonzales's story is getting exciting, so I try to focus.

"We're going to break you into smaller groups so you can fit into the different rooms of the rancho. Two groups will share a tour guide. You'll have either a regular guide or a special guide dressed in period costume, representing a type of resident of Rancho Los Cerritos. Let's go to the gate."

Henny clutches my hand. "We'd better stick together. We don't want to be separated."

We all shuffle after Mr. Gonzales. As soon as we step out from under the canopy, bright sunshine blinds me. I blink until my eyes stop hurting.

Mr. Gonzales leads us through a pretty garden. The smells of the plants are sweet and strong. After two minutes, we reach a pair of bright-green doors. *What's inside?* I wonder, and I wish I could climb them and peek over.

Mrs. Sabban divides us up into six groups: five with eight girls and one with just six. An adult stands with each group.

After I get sorted into a group with Mrs. Pelcowitz, whose daughter Yocheved is in the other fourth-grade class, I notice we've been joined by several more grown-ups. Some are dressed in casual clothing, like Mr. Gonzales wears. But a few of them are dressed in old-fashioned clothes. One woman wears a long blue cotton dress covered by an apron. A funny little hat rests on top of her gray hair, which is coiled into an enormous bun. The man next to her is wearing a white shirt with a collar, an embroidered vest, a jacket, and long slacks. There's a black thing around his neck, kind of like a tie, and a black hat on his head. It's not like the hat Dad wears, but flatter, with a wider brim. He looks like he stepped out of a photo from our California history book. Another man wears the clothes of a workman: rumpled overalls, boots, and an old, stained hat. He's got a cheery red bandanna around his neck.

I hope our group doesn't get one of those silly-looking interpreters. They'll probably act like they're people from the past. Which is also silly. They're normal people, in the here and now, just like me.

Mr. Gonzales introduces each of them. And then the scruffy workman — Kyle Williams — moseys over to our group and Mrs. Sabban's.

"Howdy," he says. "Are you ready?"

I'm not. I'm hot and bored.

He sticks a key in the lock of the green door on the right. When it swings open, it reveals a big, beautiful house with green trim and a garden with beautiful trees and flowers. And I hear the sound of water; is it a fountain? I want to run inside and find out!

Maybe this won't be so boring after all.

CHAPTER 6

Splash!

Our tour guide leads us through the green door and waits till we are all gathered together. Then he says, "In case you didn't hear Mr. Gonzales's introduction, my name is Mr. Williams, and I am a shepherd working at the Bixby ranch in 1873." I roll my eyes at Henny, as if to say, *Shepherd? Riiiiight.* She grins.

Mr. Williams opens his arms wide. "This here is what we call the inner courtyard. Back when Rancho Los Cerritos was used for cattle farming and sheep herding, this area was trampled every day by the family, ranch hands, and animals. Over there," he gestures to one wing of the building, "is the blacksmith's shop, the foreman's residence, the laundry, and a storeroom. We'll peek into those before we tour the main residence."

Now he points at the lawn, toward the pond. It's shaped like a swimming pool, but there are plants growing in it!

"In the 1930s, the house was fixed up for the Bixby family by a landscape architect named Ralph Cornell. He decided to repurpose what had been a practical space for pleasure and beauty. He put in this garden, complete with a pond. The pink flowers are water lilies."

Something flies by my face, very close. As I jump back, all I see is a shimmer of blue. "What was that?!"

Mr. Williams laughs. "Dragonfly. The pond attracts a lot of them."

He turns around and starts leading everyone toward the far side of the rancho. Everyone follows, but I can't take my eyes off the pond.

"What's the frog thing?" I point to a strange sculpture at the edge of the pond.

Turning around, Mr. Williams says, "It pours fresh water from its mouth."

"What's it made of?" Leora asks.

"Brass." He looks around at us. "Any more questions before we move on?"

Everyone is silent. As they walk away, I creep closer to the pond. And closer. *I wonder if there are any fish in there...*

I lean over to look, and my headband slips into the water. "Eeek!"

One of the girls hears me and turns around. "Adina!"

Other people turn around to see what she noticed.

"What's wrong?" Mrs. Pelcowitz asks.

"My headband! It fell in the water!"

Her hand slaps her forehead as Mr. Williams doubles back. "Something wrong?" he asks.

Can I just melt into the ground like a week-old snowman, please? "Um…um…my headband? It fell in the water."

His hand slaps his forehead too. I guess I have that effect on people. "We'll fish it out later."

"But it's my favorite headband!" I blurt out.

At first, he just stares at me. Then he leans over the edge too, to get a better look.

And his dirty old hat falls off his head, straight into the mucky pond water.

"Oh no!" Mrs. Pelcowitz's eyes widen in horror. Half the girls make big o's with their mouths, some covering them with their hands.

Mr. Williams looks at me, and then at the pond, where his hat is now floating. Again at me, again at the pond. Then he scoops the hat out of the water. Rolling up his right sleeve, he says, "And now for the favorite headband." He lies down next to the pond, reaches in, and starts poking around.

"Aha!" He pulls out my headband and holds it over his head.

Gingerly, I take it from him. It is wet, and something green and totally gross is trailing from the blue bow. Henny appears at my elbow.

"Maybe you can wash it?" She smiles one of those smiles someone flashes you when they know things are bad but they're trying to pretend otherwise.

I look at the headband doubtfully.

Meanwhile, Mr. Williams has risen to his feet. "All right, then. Let's head for the blacksmith's shop."

As he walks away, I notice there's green slime on the edge of his hat.

CHAPTER 7

Touchy-Feely

Mr. Williams leads us to a door off the inner courtyard; it's painted the same green as the gate. But before we can enter, he stops and faces us. "If I came to your house and I entered your room, what would you want me to do?"

Several girls raise their hands, and he picks Tania Warsaw. "Play chess?"

Everyone laughs, even Mr. Williams. After a minute, he says, "I'm rather fond of chess, but I was looking for a different answer." He points to someone else.

"Keep your hands off my stuff!" Shoshi says, shaking a finger at him.

"That's right!" he says, then takes us all in with a long glance. "When you go inside, keep your hands to yourselves unless I invite you to touch something."

I start to get nervous because my fingers itch to touch things. My mother complains about it every time I go shopping with her. *Adina, can you please look but not touch?!* Wishing for a pocket to stick my hand in, I settle for making both hands into fists at my sides.

"And," Mr. Williams adds, "when you walk, don't drag or shuffle your feet. Lift them high, like this." He shows us with his own booted feet. "You'll see why when we go inside. Also, get a good look at the walls when you go inside. They're two feet thick! That's because they're made of big adobe bricks. A room like the one we're about to enter would be made from about a thousand of those bricks."

He turns around and steps inside. The doorway is so low, he nearly has to duck as he enters. We all follow and try to make room for everyone by walking as far inside as we can. There's a bed, a rack on the wall with a hat and whips hanging on it, and a table with two chairs. Near the head of the bed, there's a china pitcher and bowl, a lamp, and a hairbrush.

"Look down." We all follow directions. The floor is made of dirt! "Why do you think I asked you to lift your feet when you walk?"

He chooses Ilana Parisi to answer. "If you dragged your feet, you could dig holes in the dirt."

"Right! If that happens, the only way to smooth it out again is to pour cow's blood all over the dirt floor."

"Ewwww!" We all squeal and wrinkle our noses.

As soon as everyone is inside, Mr. Williams says, "This is the *mah-yur do-mo*'s room."

"The what?" I call out.

"It's spelled like 'major domo.' It's Spanish for 'foreman,' the person who manages all the workers on the farm." Swiveling to take in everyone, he goes on. "During the Temple period, most of the workers at Rancho Los Cerritos were Mexican. And this was actually part of Mexico until…" He grins. "Anyone remember the name of the war after which California became part of the US?"

We learned that in school, so a whole lot of girls raise their hands. He calls on Chaya Sarah. "The Mexican-American War."

"Perfect! Remember the date?"

She squishes up her face like she's thinking hard, then says, "1846?"

"You got it! During the war, John Temple — who had become Mexican and even called himself Don Juan — was arrested and locked in his own house. When the Americans came, they let him out. What they didn't know was that John's wife, who was Mexican, had been buying gunpowder and munitions for the Mexicans!"

We laugh, and Mr. Williams goes on. "Anyway, the

major domo — unlike the rest of the workers — had his own room and it doubled as his office. Over on the table, you can see a ledger. That's where he kept track of how many hides he'd delivered to be shipped back east, and how many pounds of tallow — that's beef fat — he'd shipped to South America. Anyone know what they do with tallow?"

When none of the girls answer, Mrs. Sabban raises her hand. "You make candles, right?"

"That's one thing. If you look up, you'll see some tallow candles in the chandelier above our heads."

I look up. "That's a chandelier?!" It looks more like two planks of wood nailed together and hung from the ceiling. The candles are yellowish and unlit.

Mrs. Pelcowitz and a couple of the girls look annoyed, but Mr. Williams snickers. "You're used to fancy ones just dripping with crystals, right?"

"Uh-huh."

"Back in those days, they didn't have electricity, and it wasn't just rich people who needed light inside their homes. Simple people had simple chandeliers."

Leaning over, he flips back the corner of the bedspread. "Anyone ever hear the expression, 'Sleep tight, don't let the bedbugs bite'?" Most of us raise our hands. "Anyone ever wonder what that means?" Again we raise our hands. "Notice what's holding up this mattress?"

We all crane our necks to get a good look. It's ropes!

"If you let your mattress sag, you'll get a backache, so it's important to tighten these ropes before you go to bed at night if they're too loose." Mr. Williams pokes the mattress. "And this mattress is stuffed with straw. You replace the straw regularly to ensure you have no bedbugs."

I start scratching just at the thought.

Mr. Williams picks up a lump of something brown and waxy from the window ledge behind him. "This is what tallow soap looks like. Anyone want to touch it?" Most of the girls shake their heads. I guess they think beef fat is disgusting. But since I've touched raw beef plenty of times while helping my parents in the kitchen, I don't really get it. When I get my turn, it has the same waxy feel as a candle. I sniff it; it's not yummy smelling like my soap at home, but it's not gross either.

After Mr. Williams shows us a few more things, we move on.

CHAPTER 8

In Disgrace

We squeeze into the next room. There's all sorts of tubs and bottles crammed into the space. To the left, there are clothes hanging from a clothesline!

"This is the laundry room as it appeared during the Bixbys' lifetimes. You'll notice the tubs and the washboards and the wringer." Mr. Williams turns a crank on the wringer. "The Bixbys hired two Chinese women — Ying and Phan — to wash their laundry and do their cooking. Ying and Phan spent all day Monday washing everyone's clothes and linens, and all Tuesday ironing them." He picks up an iron and demonstrates how it was heated and used. "We're going to pass this around. Make sure it comes back to me at the end." He pauses, then adds, "You might want to use two hands."

Elisheva reaches toward him, and when he places the iron in her hands, she almost drops it. It's so comical that a couple girls laugh. "It's heavy!" Elisheva tells them, sounding defensive.

She passes the iron to Sigal, who nods in agreement.

"It's heavy," Mr. Williams explains, "because it's made of iron."

Henny hands me the iron. It's so heavy. I hold it out to Zeesie, but she only extends one hand to me. She takes it and…

Bong!

…it lands an inch from her foot.

I reach out to Zeesie, whose eyes have gone very, very wide. "Are you okay?!"

Zeesie gulps, then looks me in the face. "It just missed me!"

Mrs. Pelcowitz rushes to her side. "*Baruch Hashem!*" She looks at me out of the corner of her eye before adding, "That could have broken your toe!"

Mr. Williams's face is pale as he crosses the room, squats down, and picks up the iron. "Has everyone had a turn?" A couple girls haven't, and he places the iron briefly into each of their hands. Then he puts it on the trivet on the counter.

He tells us some more about the laundry, but it's hard

to pay attention. Mrs. Pelcowitz and Shoshi and a couple of the other girls keep looking at me as if I'd caused the accident. As if I'd done something wrong.

But I hadn't. Really, I hadn't!

Looking around the room, the clothes on the clothesline catch my eye. There's a long-sleeved button-down shirt, a lovely slip trimmed in lace, and a little girl's dress. Creeping closer, I look up to admire the dress. It's purple, with lovely flowers. Without realizing it, I reach up to touch the smooth fabric…

"Young lady!" Mr. Williams's face is deep red. "Get your hand off that!"

I pull away. "Sorry, it's just—" I don't know how to explain the way my hand just wants to touch things all the time, like it has its own brain.

Mr. Williams takes three deep breaths. "Mrs. Sabban?"

She makes her way over to him. "Yes?"

"This young lady has been a little too enthusiastic with the displays. And this is the third problem we've had this morning with her."

Mrs. Sabban's face pales. "I'm sorry."

"I know she's not trying to cause trouble, but I think we should have her wait outside. If she keeps at it, I'm afraid she's going to get hurt, or maybe damage some of the property." His hand wanders to his hat, which he takes off and then settles back on his head.

Mr. Williams wants to send me out of the rancho? Where are they going to send me? "But...but...I didn't mean it!"

Mrs. Sabban looks at me with a sympathetic look on her face. Resting a hand on my shoulder, she says, "Can you give her another chance?"

Mr. Williams shakes his head. "I don't think that's wise. We need to keep the children safe and the exhibits intact so all the visitors can enjoy them."

Mrs. Sabban bites her lip. Then she says, "I guess one of the parents will have to take her back to the bus, or something. I can't leave her unattended." She turns to Mrs. Pelcowitz. "Since our groups are already together, I'll send you to wait at the bus with Adina. I think Shirley is there."

"But you can't send me to the bus!" I scream. "I got my permission slip signed! I sent in the money! I wrote that letter to Mrs. Rubin!"

Mrs. Sabban takes a step away from me. "Adina, I would appreciate it if you calmed down."

"Calm down?!" How can she ask me to calm down?

"It's time to go."

"I don't want to go."

"You're making a scene."

Looking left and right, I see she's right. Girls are looking at me with disgust and frustration.

Mrs. Sabban catches my eye. "Maybe if you calm down and take a little break, we can invite you back."

Reluctantly, I turn to go. Mr. Williams explains to Mrs. Pelcowitz how to get out of the ranch building without unlocking the green gate. We walk quickly through the main building, without getting more than a glimpse of the shiny windows, old furniture, and many, many books, then we exit through a small parking lot. She tries to talk to me, but I just ignore her. I've made a fool of myself. I know it. All the girls will remember my tantrum when they look back at this field trip. The shame burns my face. Why can't I just learn to control myself?

CHAPTER 9

Mr. Gonzales

I'm trembling as Mrs. Pelcowitz walks me back to the bus. We pass the Visitor Center, the sign. Is my nose dripping? I wipe my face with my sleeve just in case.

It's even hotter than before the tour, and every step I take kicks up dirt. My uniform feels itchy. And my nose won't stop dripping.

"Here," Mrs. Pelcowitz says. "I've got a tissue." Fishing around in her purse, she eventually pulls out one of those neat little packages. However, the tissue she hands me is too rough. Yuck!

Reaching the bus, we discover the door is closed. Mrs. Pelcowitz peers inside through the window and taps on the glass.

"Shirley mentioned sitting on the picnic benches," I say. "Do you know where the picnic benches are?"

Mrs. Pelcowitz pulls back and takes the map of the rancho out of her sweater pocket. Unfolding it, she looks for the picnic area. "It should be in the California Native Garden."

We trudge along the path suggested by the map, passing lots of plants along the way. Their scents tickle my nose, and I have to wiggle it so I don't sneeze. We skirt around the edge of the adobe too. It's pretty, with green-painted balconies. I hear one of the tour guides telling the kids about the kitchen.

Mrs. Pelcowitz must have heard it too. "I wish I'd gotten a good look inside," she says.

"Maybe you can come some other time."

"I wouldn't have to if you'd just behaved properly."

I stop feeling sad and start getting angry. I didn't cause her trouble on purpose! And why does she have to complain? I'm already being punished!

After a couple minutes, we find some picnic tables. This must be the place.

"You need something?" a voice says behind us.

I turn around. It's Shirley, sitting on a picnic bench in the shade with a bottle of water. She still looks warm and friendly. But why does she now sound so worried?

"No," Mrs. Pelcowitz says. "We just need a little break."

"Me too," she says.

"Is something wrong, Shirley?" I ask.

Mrs. Pelcowitz shoots me a look like she doesn't think I should be talking but doesn't know how to make me stop.

"Do you see that man over there?" Shirley's looking at a man seated a couple tables over.

It's Mr. Gonzales, the man who met us at the bus. "What about him?"

"When I went to say hi, he sounded funny."

"Funny?" I ask.

Shirley takes a sip of her water as she thinks of how to explain. "His words are all…slurred. Like they run together."

Remembering the flyer in my father's car, I start to march towards Mr. Gonzales.

"Adina!" Mrs. Pelcowitz grabs my arm.

I shrug her off, and now Shirley joins me. When we reach Mr. Gonzales, she says, "Mister, are you sure you're okay?"

"I don' feel so good. Maybe I'm cummin' down wif sumfin'." He's clutching his head.

I'm looking at Mr. Gonzales's face now, and it looks different — lopsided almost.

That's when I remember the thingy from Dad's car, the infographic. "Mr. Gonzales, can you please look at me and smile?"

"A-*dee*-nah!" Mrs. Pelcowitz says. "That's enough! Why can't you just leave him alone? If he says he's not feeling well, maybe he just needs a little rest here in the shade."

I look at Shirley and then back at Mrs. Pelcowitz. I whisper, "I'm worried."

"What are you talking about?"

I gesture for her to bend down. Reluctantly, she leans over. I whisper in her ear, "I think Mr. Gonzales is having a stroke."

Shirley adds, "So do I. This is what my auntie looked like when she had one."

"What?!" Mrs. Pelcowitz's eyebrows drop low and she stares at me with disbelief. "How would you know that?"

"There are signs," I say, motioning for Mrs. Pelcowitz to keep her voice down. "Signs a person might be having a stroke. You remember them with…" I think back to the car. "FAST. Face, arms, smile, tongue. If they flunk the test, you call 911."

"Don't be ridiculous!" Mrs. Pelcowitz puts her hands on her hips. "There's nothing wrong with Mr. Gonzales. You're just making trouble, just like you've made trouble the whole day."

"That's unfair!" I burst into tears. "This is different. It's not about me! It's about Mr. Gonzales."

At this point, we are so loud that Mr. Gonzales can't help but pay attention. "Whuh 'bow me?" He struggles to stand, but his feet scrabble in the sand and pebbles. He sags back onto the bench. "Girlie, don' worry 'bow me."

Shirley rests a hand on my back. "How do you do

the test?"

Walking over to Mr. Gonzales, I say, "Hey, I want to check you to see if something serious is wrong. Can you smile at me?"

Instead of the friendly smile he had given us when we arrived at the rancho, the right side of his smile is higher than the other, just a bit. Then he says, his voice quavering in addition to slurring, "You think I'm havin' a stroke?"

I nod.

"I thaw, maybe…" Tears slip from his eyes. "Been having problems with my blood pressure…"

"Can you raise both your arms in front of you, as high as they can go?" I show him what I mean by doing it myself. And then he does it, but his right arm is higher than the left.

"Can you raise that one," Mrs. Pelcowitz points to the left one, "any higher?" Her voice is high-pitched with panic. I know how she feels, because I'm scared now, very scared.

Mr. Gonzales tries. "No." A wrinkle appears above his eyebrows.

"Okay," I say, "stick out your tongue."

Shirley looks at me. She already has one hand on her cell phone. After a pause, Mr. Gonzales does it. And his tongue curves to one side.

"I'm calling 911," Mrs. Pelcowitz says. She digs in her purse, but Shirley has already dialed before Mrs. Pelcowitz finds her phone.

CHAPTER 10

Just in Time

While we wait for the ambulance to arrive, I hold one of Mr. Gonzales's hands, and Shirley holds the other. It's only about four or five minutes before we hear the sirens approach. Mrs. Pelcowitz runs out to show the paramedics where their patient is.

As she comes back with two of them, one male and one female, a woman dressed in an old-fashioned costume comes out of the Visitor Center. "What's going on?"

Shirley tells him, "One of your workers is having a stroke. At least we think he is."

Her eyes go big. "You're with the school group, right? I'll go tell your teachers. Then I'll be right back." She rushes back into the building.

"Which one's the patient?" the male paramedic asks.

Mrs. Pelcowitz rushes to Mr. Gonzales's side. "Here. His name is Mr. Gonzales."

"Mmmmarrrtin Gon-gon-zalessss," he says.

"How long has his speech been slurred like that?"

Shirley shrugs.

"I noticed it about ten minutes ago," I say.

The other paramedic turns toward me as she sets down a big box of equipment and unsnaps the lid. She says, "And you are…?"

"Adina Ben Ami. And this is Shirley. She drove our class here."

Shirley interrupted, "I noticed Mr. Gonzales didn't sound right—"

"And then, when she mentioned it, I thought maybe he was having a stroke!"

The paramedic smiles at me. "We'll take a look and see."

The other paramedic tells Mrs. Pelcowitz and me to step back so they can examine Mr. Gonzales without interruption. In addition to repeating the FAST test, they check his blood pressure and temperature. They put a sensor on his finger. It beeps when Mr. Gonzales's heart beats. I remember seeing that once when I went to the emergency room. In voices too low for us to overhear, the paramedics talk to each other, rapid fire.

Abruptly, the first paramedic stands. He starts talking

into a walkie-talkie as he hurries back to the ambulance.

The second one says, "Shirley, Adina, you were smart to call us."

I realize then that Mr. Gonzales is in real danger! Again I start to cry.

Shirley gives my hand a quick squeeze and says, "We made a good team."

When Mrs. Pelcowitz comes over to comfort me, I burrow right into her shoulder. Her sweater is soft, fuzzy. It smells faintly of some kind of perfume, maybe roses.

The first paramedic comes back, pushing a rolling metal gurney, and the two paramedics together load Mr. Gonzales onto it. They start to hook up equipment for him, even as they head back to the ambulance. Chasing after them, we have to hustle to keep up. After they've loaded him into the back, the female paramedic looks over to us.

Shirley says, "Well, now. This trip has not exactly gone as I expected."

At that moment, Mrs. Friend shows up, the woman in the old-fashioned dress at her elbow. "I heard there was an emergency."

Rubbing my back, Mrs. Pelcowitz says, "Mr. Gonzales appears to have had a stroke."

Mrs. Friend's face goes pale.

It doesn't take long to get Mr. Gonzales ready to go

to the hospital. The female paramedic comes out of the bus and hops into the passenger seat of the ambulance. The male paramedic climbs out of the back and into the driver's seat. Just a second later, the sirens begin to blare all over again, and the ambulance pulls out of the parking lot at full speed.

We stand there, speechless, for what seems the longest time.

"I'd better deal with the students," Mrs. Friend says, eventually. But she doesn't budge. She stares with wide eyes at nothing in particular.

"You two saved her," Mrs. Pelcowitz says. She also seems stunned.

Mrs. Friend turns toward her. "What?"

"Shirley and Adina," she says, her voice getting stronger, "saved Mr. Gonzales. First, Shirley noticed that he didn't look right…didn't sound right. Then Adina told me — insisted — that we had to help."

"I had a hunch," said Shirley, "but Adina knew just what to do."

Everyone looks at me.

"How did you know what was wrong, Adina?" Mrs. Friend asks.

I shift from one foot to another, uncomfortable with everyone's attention. "My father. He had this thing in the car, an infographic, he called it. It explained the signs of a stroke."

After a second, I add, "I saw it just this morning, on the way to school."

"That's like…Heavenly intervention, ma'am," Shirley says.

I nod. It was Heavenly intervention. Not just Shirley, not just me. It was God too.

Finally, Mrs. Friend walks back to the main building so she can find the rest of the students.

AFTER FORTY-FIVE MINUTES, the kids and teachers and moms come streaming out of the Visitor Center. Some of the girls must have brought money, because they have little bags in their hands labeled "Friends of Rancho Los Cerritos."

Mrs. Friend and Mrs. Pelcowitz have been heaping praise on me. And the moment they tell the girls what happened, the girls start in. Leora throws her arms around me like we're best friends or something and declares, "You're a hero!"

"Heroine," I correct her, as I drag her arms off me.

A few more girls come over to celebrate with me, and it bugs me — *really* bugs me. First of all, it wasn't just me; it was Shirley too. Second, it's like they think I'm one person when I do bad stuff and another person when I do good stuff. And they only like the me who does good.

I feel a hand on my sleeve, and it startles me. "You okay?"

Looking up, I see Henny, with a worried look on her face. "You seem a little out of it," she adds.

It's nice to have someone worry about me instead of piling on compliments. "I'm just nervous. What if Mr. Gonzales doesn't get better?"

Henny hugs me. "What if he does?"

"Do you realize," I say, "that if I'd been good this morning, kept my hands to myself, been able to stay with the tour group, I would never have been in the picnic area?"

She winks at me. "I think we're all in the right place at the right time — God put us here! But not everyone does what we're supposed to do in that place and time."

"Shirley would still have been there…but I guess you have a point."

Thinking about this, I follow her back onto the bus. We sit together again, but this time we don't count cars. Henny tells me about the rest of the ranch house, the neat kitchen with the old icebox, and the porch where the Bixby family served all the ranch hands. She explains how to play hoops, which they were allowed to do after their picnic lunch. I realize then that I forgot to eat lunch. My stomach rumbles.

"Mrs. Sabban," I say across the aisle, "I never ate lunch."

"You must be starving!" she exclaims. Popping the lid off the cooler, she finds my paper lunch bag. She leans forward to talk to Shirley. "Since Adina was busy helping you rescue Mr. Gonzales" — I roll my eyes — "is it okay for her to eat on the bus? She forgot to eat when all the drama happened."

"No problem, ma'am."

The brown paper crumples in my hands when she gives me the bag. Some of the paper is tearing because of the wetness around my melting juice box. I pull my juice out of the bag, unwrap the straw, and poke it in the box. As I take the first sip, Henny nudges her open bag of popcorn chips along the ugly vinyl seat toward me.

"I saved some for you," she whispers.

CHAPTER 11

The Best Adina

Someone must have called ahead, because the principal runs out to meet the bus as we pull up outside. Everyone wants to hug me and tell me how proud she is of me. I tell her that it wasn't just me; it was Shirley too — and Heavenly intervention.

On my way down the bus steps, Shirley says, "Keep up the good work, Adina!" She looks like she wants to say more, but her eyes fill with tears and her smile goes kind of wiggly. Waving, I walk out the exit.

I'm tired. A peek at the clock tells me we've got an hour and a half left of school.

Heaving a sigh, I shuffle back to class with everyone else. I'm not sure what the teachers expect us to do after our field trip. All the girls are buzzing with excitement, talking about the rancho, talking about me, Shirley, and Mr. Gonzales. Nothing's going to get done.

I plop into my seat and put my head down on my desk.

A moment later, the phone hanging on our wall rings, and Mrs. Sabban picks it up. "Adina. Your mother is here. She's taking you home for the rest of the day."

As I pack my backpack with the remains of my lunch, I wonder who let my mother know what had happened. Whoever did it, I'm grateful. And I'm grateful to my mother for coming to get me. Normally on a Thursday afternoon, she's seeing patients.

Mom is waiting for me when I reach the lobby. She moves toward me like she wants to rush over and hug me, but she stops herself. She knows I'm not usually the huggy-huggy type.

Today, however, I could really use a hug, so I run to her.

As soon as her arms close around me, I start crying again. I've lost count of the number of times I've cried today. For sure I've never cried so many times since I was a baby. At the rate I'm going, I'll be able to water the lawn with all my tears.

"Shhh…it's okay. It's okay, Adina." Soft fingers stroke my hair and back.

My voice is muffled against Mom's collarbone. "But

what if Mr. Gonzales dies?"

"He's not going to die. The principal got a phone call from the rancho a few minutes ago."

I let go of Mom. "She did?"

Mom nodded. "Mr. Gonzales is going to be just fine. He'll need some therapy, and more medicine, but he's going to be okay."

My heart smiles first, and then I feel it reach my face.

"They left the name of the hospital. The principal wrote it down for me. I was thinking that maybe we'll go visit him on Sunday. They expect he'll be there at least until Monday."

Mom takes my backpack from me and slings it over her shoulder. I grab her hand like when I was small, and we walk to the car together. "I'd like that, Mom."

The traffic out on La Brea Avenue is loud, but we turn and then we're heading down a side street lined with sycamores. The leaves are unfurling, green and hopeful, and squirrels are zipping along the branches.

Suddenly, it occurs to me that Mom hasn't complimented me for helping Mr. Gonzales. And, strangely, that makes me happy. It takes me a moment before I realize why: Mom is not surprised. It's like she's believed all along that I'm capable of saving someone.

My mother didn't pick me up from school because I am a heroine. She picked me up because she knew I would be feeling jittery and muddled and would want to be away from all the people making a fuss over me at school.

Stopping at her minivan, Mom clicks the remote and all the locks pop. "Want ice cream, or should we go straight home?"

"Straight home."

Before I duck into the minivan, I make sure to hug her one more time.

While we drive past familiar stucco houses, I think about how mad I was at Mom and Dad last night. I thought that maybe they didn't love me. For sure they don't like some of the things I do.

Are people and the things they do the same thing?

Remembering that little "chat" in the den, the hurt I felt feels fresh. But maybe people *are* separate from the things they do. It really is true that I do things that bother people; sometimes they bother me! But I know I'm a good person.

Maybe my parents do love me, and know I'm good deep inside, and that's why they want to help.

I wait until we drive a couple more blocks before saying, "When we get home, can we schedule that appointment? To get me tested?"

Mom's reflection looks startled in her rearview mirror. "Sure, honey."

I smile and lean back. "And one more thing."

"What?"

"Can we get sushi for dinner?"

Acknowledgments

I owe several people a tremendous debt of gratitude for their assistance with this project. For her cheerleading, proofreading, and advice, I thank Devorah Talia Gordon. For daily check-ins and support, I thank Merri Ukraincik, Nina Badzin, and all the other women in Nina's "High Five" group during National Novel Writing Month (NaNoWriMo) in 2017.

For guiding our family on our most recent tour of Rancho Los Cerritos, and for putting up with our extensive (and excessive) questions, I thank Terry Barber and the rest of the rancho's staff. If you happen to be in Southern California, you can pay them a visit yourselves in Long Beach. Any mistakes in the descriptions of Rancho Los Cerritos or its history are entirely my own.

I thank my husband, Daniel, and our children — Aryeh, Paltiel, Ahuva, and Hodaya — for tolerating my preoccupation as I wrote this book. And for accompanying me to Rancho Los Cerritos on a Sunday when they could have been doing other things.

Thanks also to Chaya Baila Lieber for her eye to detail and for preventing me from looking bad on the page, and to Yocheved Nadell for the spunky Adina we see on the cover.

And — as always — I thank the Ribbono shel Olam for sending me ideas, popping solutions to problems into my head, and everything else He does as the Author of this entire universe.

About the Author

Rebecca Klempner's previous books include *Glixman in a Fix* (Menucha Publishers, 2017), *Mazal's Luck Runs Out* (CreateSpace, 2015), and *A Dozen Daisies for Raizy* (Hachai Publishing, 2008). She lives and writes in Los Angeles. Although she has visited Rancho Los Cerritos several times, she has yet to be sent home early.